First published by Parragon in 2012

Parragon
Queen Street House
4 Queen Street
Bath BA1 1HE, UK
www.parragon.com

ISBN 978-1-4454-9329-9

Printed in China

Sleep Little Angel

PaRragon

Bath • New York • Singapore • Hong Kong • Cologne • Delhi
Melbourne • Amsterdam • Johannesburg • Shenzhen

Sleep little angel,
And never you cry.
Spring will come,
And spring will pass by.

And while it passes, I will sing
Of birds and primroses yellow in spring.

I will sing of the violet,
Lest you forget,
Lest you forget,
My little one, the spring.

Sleep little angel,
The buzzing fly
Will soar in the summer that passes by.
Summer is here all wild and green,
And I will sing of the flowering bean.

I will sing of the firefly,
Lest you forget,
Lest you forget,
The summer that is not ended yet.

Sleep little angel,
This frosty night,
Fall has come,
Birds take their flight.

But I will sing of this same cold air,
The smell of chrysanthemums everywhere.

I will sing of the falling leaves,
Lest you forget,
Lest you forget,
The fall of the year is not ended yet.

Sleep little angel,
The sun goes down,
The snow is white on the frozen ground.

The snow is soft, and softly I'll sing
Of stars and every quiet thing.

I will sing of tall black trees that fret,
Lest you forget,
Lest you forget,
The ice and snow are not melted yet.

Sleep little angel, and I will sing
Of summer and winter and fall and spring,
Of stars and every quiet thing,
Of frost and primroses I will sing.